To Hedy

from

Love Kellog

THE
MYSTERIOUS
TADPOLE

STEVEN KELLOGG

DIAL BOOKS FOR YOUNG READERS

NEW YORK

Published by
Dial Books for Young Readers
A Division of Penguin Books USA Inc.
375 Hudson Street
New York, New York 10014
Copyright © 1977 by Steven Kellogg
All rights reserved
Typography by Atha Tehon
Printed in Hong Kong by South China Printing Co.
COBE
12   14   15   13   11

Library of Congress Cataloging in Publication Data
Kellogg, Steven.
The mysterious tadpole.
Summary: It soon becomes clear that Louis's pet
tadpole is not turning into an ordinary frog.
[1. Pets—Fiction] I. Title.
PZ7.K292Mw   [E]   77-71517
ISBN 0-8037-6245-3   ISBN 0-8037-6246-1 lib. bdg.

For Joseph

Uncle McAllister lived in Scotland. Every year he sent Louis a birthday gift for his nature collection.

"This is the best one yet!" cried Louis.

The next day he took his entire collection to school for show-and-tell.

"Class, this is a tadpole," said Mrs. Shelbert. She asked Louis to bring it back often so they could all watch it become a frog.

Louis named the tadpole Alphonse. Every day Alphonse
ate several cheeseburgers.

Louis found that he was eager to learn.

When Alphonse became too big for his jar, Louis moved him to the sink.

After Alphonse outgrew the sink, Louis's parents agreed to let him use the bathtub.

One day Mrs. Shelbert decided that Alphonse was not turning into an ordinary frog.

She asked Louis to stop bringing him to school.

By the time summer vacation arrived, Alphonse was enormous.

"He's too big for the bathtub," said Louis's mother.

"He's too big for the apartment," said Louis's father.

"He needs a swimming pool," said Louis.

"There is no place in our apartment for a swimming pool," said his parents.

Louis suggested that they buy the parking lot next door
and build a swimming pool.

"It would cost more money than we have," said his parents.
"Your tadpole will have to be donated to the zoo."
The thought of Alphonse in a cage made Louis very sad.

Then, in the middle of the night, Louis remembered that the junior high had a swimming pool that nobody used during the summer.

Louis hid Alphonse under a rug and smuggled him into the school.

After making sure that Alphonse felt at home, Louis went back to bed.

Every morning Louis spent several hours swimming with his friend. In the afternoon he earned the money for Alphonse's cheeseburgers by delivering newspapers.

Meanwhile the training continued. Alphonse learned to retrieve things from the bottom of the pool.

Summer vacation passed quickly. Louis worried what would happen to Alphonse now that school had reopened.

As soon as the first day ended, he ran to the junior high. The students were getting ready for after-school activities.

Louis arrived just as the first swimming race began.

Alphonse was delighted to see all the swimmers.

"It's a submarine from another planet!" bellowed the coach. "Call the police! Call the Navy!"

"No! It's a tadpole!" cried Louis. "He's my pet!"

The coach was upset and confused.
"You have until tomorrow," he cried, "to get that creature out of the pool!"

Louis didn't know what to do. On the way home he met his friend Miss Seevers, the librarian, and he told her his problem.

Miss Seevers went back to the junior high school with Louis, but when she saw Alphonse, she was so shocked that she dropped her purse and the books she was carrying into the swimming pool. Alphonse retrieved them.

Then Miss Seevers telephoned Louis's Uncle McAllister in Scotland. He told her that he had caught the little tadpole in Loch Ness, a large lake near his cottage.

Miss Seevers said, "I'm convinced that your uncle has given you a very rare Loch Ness monster!"

"I don't care!" cried Louis. "He's my pet, and I love him!" He begged Miss Seevers to help him raise enough money to buy the parking lot near his apartment so he could build a swimming pool for Alphonse.

Suddenly Miss Seevers had an idea.

"In 1639 there was a battle in our city's harbor," she said. "A pirate treasure ship was sunk, and no one has ever been able to find it. But perhaps we can!"

The next morning Miss Seevers and Louis rented a boat.

In the middle of the harbor Louis showed Alphonse a picture of a treasure chest.

Alphonse disappeared under the water.

Louis and Miss Seevers bought the parking lot.

They hired some helpers.

And when the pool was completed,

all the children in the city were invited to swim.

That night Louis said, "Alphonse, next week is my birthday, which means that we've been friends for almost a year."

Far away in Scotland Uncle McAllister was also thinking about the approaching birthday. While out hiking he discovered an unusual stone in a clump of grass and sticks.

"A perfect gift for my nephew!" he cried.

"I'll deliver it in person!"

Uncle McAllister arrived at Louis's apartment and gave Louis the present.

Louis couldn't wait to add it to his collection.

Suddenly a crack appeared in the stone....